THE RAM STORY

KIDS , GROWN UPS

ABU BUCKER A

Hello !!!! readers I am ABU BUCKER A and i like to write stories as a part time hobby.

I started writing this story for my friend who did not let me sleep for more than 20 days telling his story . if I fell asleep my friend would hit me and wold shake me untill i wake up and made me here tis story thanks to my other friend who came up after 20 days to fill up my place

SPECIAL THANKS TO MY FRIEND RAM FOR TELLING HIS IMAGINATION BEFORE HE GOES TO SLEEP.

Contents

Foreword

FOREWORD

GIVEN BY - ABU BUCKER A

When you start a relationship with someone stay with them , love is not something that some one must force it is a mutual relation between two individuals . They share their heart and their secrets . Love is not something that can only be shown with your girlfriend or boyfriend , it can also be shown by a mother and father to their children , a animals love towards his owner guess what the love that a god shows to a living being .

Preface

The Ram Story was the book i wrote with my friend ram who had a crush on Nit. Unfortunatelly my friend ram was unable to marry the love of his life but thtas ok as he is married to another nice girl kiru a south korean. The love story that ram wanted with nit and the adventerous life and the dream that he want to be the prince charming who would save the beautiful prince nit have been shortly descried on this book.

Acknowledgements

ITS YOU THE MOST WANTED CHARCTER SO THANKS TO YOU READERS.

Prologue

This is a totally imaginary story and some incidents are true and those names are truely taken from the starting , ending or middle three letters.

Imagine yourself as th main character of the story to fell te expirence and make the rest of the characters as your friend or relations .

True Love !!!

'DONT CARE ABOUT WHAT OTHERS THINK
ABOUT YOU BE YOURSELF A UNIQUE LOVABLE
HUMAN "
"LOSSING DOESNT MEAN GOING BACK LOSSING IS
WHAT YOU GIVE UP FOR OTHERS HAPPINESS"